For Igls

Igles means hedgehogs in German
and coincidentally is the name of
the village in Austria
which inspired this book.

Thomas
(Tom mouse's Austrian cousin)

Sam
and the other
rabbits

Edward Hedgehog
(Ed)

First Published 1992
by Brownsword Books
28 Gay Street · Bath · England BA1 2PD

Printed and bound in Great Britain

ISBN 1 873615 98 1

What happened to
Edward Hedgehog
one winter

by Kate Veale

Ed was fed up.
It was December,
the first frosts had
whitened the trees
and fields, and the
last of the leaves
had shrivelled on
the branches.
It was time for
him to hibernate,
but he did not want to because
he wanted to see what winter
was like particularly when
it snowed. So he
bought himself
some green wellies,
a scarf and gloves and
decided to stay awake
instead.

He went outside
and looked up at the sky
through the cold air
hoping for snow,
but the sky seemed very bright
and any clouds that appeared
were too flimsy and thin
to produce even the smallest
snowflake.

Disappointed
he turned
and walked
back to the
house.

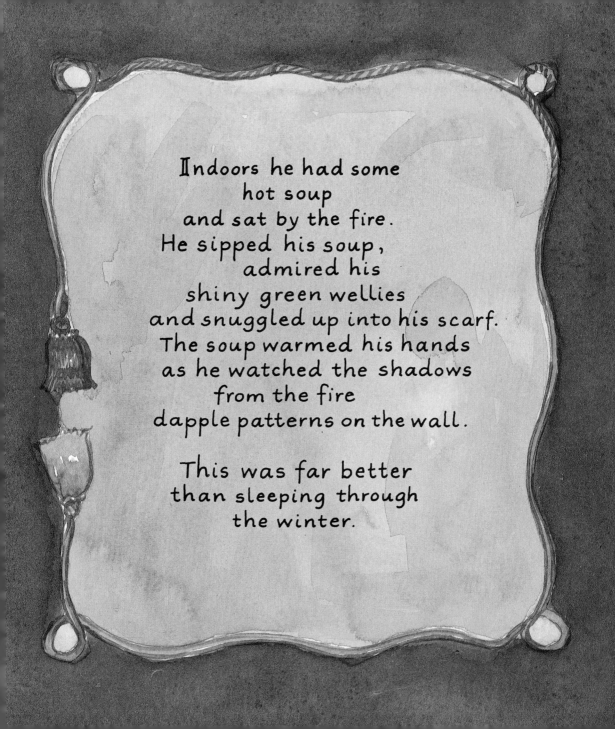

Indoors he had some
hot soup
and sat by the fire.
He sipped his soup,
admired his
shiny green wellies
and snuggled up into his scarf.
The soup warmed his hands
as he watched the shadows
from the fire
dapple patterns on the wall.

This was far better
than sleeping through
the winter.

When he went to bed each night he set all his alarm clocks because he was worried that he might not wake up in the morning. They made such a row that he was quite bad-tempered

quiet tick. quiet tick. quiet tick. quiet tick

for the first ten minutes each day but he soon cheered up after a cup of tea.

Every morning as usual he looked outside hoping that it had snowed. He was always disappointed. But then one evening as he was sitting by his fire

he thought that the night sounded quieter than usual. He opened the curtains and looked out.

It had snowed !

At last
it had
snowed
and the land lay
cold and pale in
the snowlight.
It was still snowing
fast in big soft
white shapes
so Ed hurriedly
pushed his feet
into his wellies,
heaved them on
and rushed
outside.

He stood looking up
at the millions of
  falling snowflakes
which made little cold
  wet patches on his nose
and cheeks and eyelids.

"Isn't it wonderful!"
he said out loud.

He picked up a handful
of snow and it crunched
  together into a
soft ball, which was very cold
  in his hands because
  he had forgotten to put
  on his gloves.

He went
back inside
and shut
the door,
his face
and hands
tingling from the cold.

"I can't wait until the morning,"
he said
and put the
snowball
on the table.
Then he
lit his candle
and went
up to bed.

When Ed came downstairs in the morning he looked everywhere for the snowball but he could not find it. He was too excited about the white fields and snow-heaped bushes and branches to worry about it for long though, and he rushed outside.

The snowball of course had melted!

It had snowed
even harder
during the night
and the sun was
shining in a
bright blue sky
over sparkling
white hills.

Ed went back inside
to eat his breakfast
already dressed in his
wellies and scarf,
but the end of
the scarf kept
dangling in the
marmalade
so he had to
take it off
again.

Marmalade

He was too excited
to eat much and
gulping down a last
mouthful he rushed
back outside. The
reflection of the
sunlight off the
snow was so bright
that he had to
put on his sunglasses.

Then he set off unsteadily down
the snowy bank from his home
towards the white fields beyond.
Before long he trod
on the end of his
scarf,
tripped
and rolled
down
the slope.

He rolled
and rolled and
became covered in snow
like a giant snowball,
with only his
black nose and green wellies
sticking out.
He was lying like this
when a rabbit
called Sam
found him.

Sam stood him up
on his wellies and brushed
off all the snow.

"What are you doing outside
in the snow?" he asked Ed, once he
realised who
it was.

"You're supposed
to be asleep!"

"I know"
said Ed,
spitting out
bits of
snow

"but I wanted to stay awake this winter
to see what it was like."

Ed had not realised that the snow would be so slippery, or so deep and soft and difficult to walk in.

You ought to get a toboggan or some skis "said Sam." It's great fun and you can travel miles really fast on skis."

Ed was a little doubtful about the speed, but agreed to go with Sam and book some lessons with the Ski Instructor who was an Austrian mouse called Thomas.

SKI SCHOOL

Sam and Ed set off together towards the slope where Thomas was teaching.

Thomas was a brilliant skier, having been almost born on skis. He had stowed away in a box of biscuits in the hold of an Austrian Airlines DC9 from Innsbrück, and had stayed in England with his cousin Tom Mouse because he liked it so much. He had taught most of the local mice and rabbits to ski reasonably well.

They could hear
Thomas shouting

"More for-vard!
More for-vard!"

His English
was
not very good but he
was tremendously
enthusiastic.

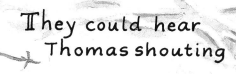

Ed put on his skis with
difficulty and
fell
straight over. He was
having trouble
standing up,
let alone
moving
forward.

Hedgehogs are not the ideal shape for skiing!

Some of the
rabbits who were
watching laughed
so much at his
efforts that they
fell in a heap.

"More for-vard,"
said Thomas again.
Ed wondered if Thomas could
actually say anything else.
"Bend ze knees,"
said Thomas.

"Definitely getting
better!" shouted
the rabbits.

Ed was pleased,
perhaps he would
learn to ski after all.

Ed was so exhausted   from his efforts
that he slept extremely well that night
after setting his alarm clocks.

Ed dreamt of
skiing down the
mountain-side at night by lamplight.

The next morning
the rabbits were already on the slopes
when Ed arrived. They all had their
skis on and started to show Ed what
they could do. They were good,
especially at little jumps.
It made Ed slightly nervous,
being a hedgehog he was not
very good at jumping.

Before long though
Thomas had Ed skiing
slowly and rather
wobbily down
the slope.

After a few days Ed was good enough to go off for the day with Sam and the other rabbits.

Thomas led the party but some of the naughtier rabbits tried to overtake him at times, mostly wildly out of control.

"Zees is not good!" said Thomas severely

and stopped.

They were in a snowy clearing surrounded by dark firs with bright sunlight slanting through the trees. The snow sparkled where the sun shone on it.

"Now ve can try a jump", said Thomas.

All the rabbits cheered, but Ed did not feel too enthusiastic. He was only just keeping up at the back.

"I vill show you,"
said Thomas, "Votch!"

The rabbits
thought that they knew it all
already of course. Thomas
showed them the snow bump

with a drop the other side.

There was quite a
lot of flat snow to land on
and trees beyond.

"Zees is ze jump.   Ready?"

The rabbits
cheered again   and Ed
                                smiled weakly.
                                His knees were
                          beginning to feel
                                wobbily.
Thomas whizzed off towards the snow bump,
flew up into the air in a perfect star jump
landed and swooshed round to stop.
        He waved his ski sticks.

        "Come!" he shouted
                but the first rabbit was
already hurtling towards the jump,
squealing with delight.

Up in the air
he went,
   awkward
   and
      off balance.

He landed
on his nose
in the
soft snow.

The next naughty rabbit
almost landed
      on top of him.

"Stop it!" shouted Thomas,
   "vait your turn.
      It's dangerous!"

The rabbits
stood chastised,
tried to behave
and took turns
to jump. Then it was time
for Ed to have a go.

"Come!" shouted Thomas
again and the rabbits
waved him on.

Ed swallowed hard.
He felt he was much too
frightened to jump.

"I can't stop now"
he said to himself.
He shut his eyes
and started towards
the snow bump.

He was so scared
when he took off

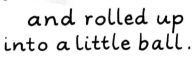

that he did
what all
frightened
hedgehogs do
and rolled up
into a little ball.

d did three perfect somersaults,
ded on his feet and fell over.

mazing!" said Thomas, amazed.

The rabbits went wild with excitement.
Ed showed definite signs of a champion in
the making.

That evening they sat around the table in Ed's kitchen drinking hot chocolate with frothy

cream floating on top and eating baked potatoes with cheese. They made plans for Ed to win the winter ski jump championships until it was time for them to go home.

Upstairs as Ed lay back in his soft bed he was overcome with tiredness. "Night," he said to no-one in particular, and fell fast asleep with his eyes tightly shut and a little smile on his happy face.

Outside
the snow fell softly
and the land froze
colder in the quiet night.
Everyone stayed
inside
in the warm
and slept.

The next morning when the time came for meeting together, everyone arrived except for Ed. The others waited in the cold warming up, ready for the first ski run of the day.

"Where is he?" they exclaimed.

After a while Sam said he would go to Ed's house to see if he was there. "I won't be long," he said. "I expect he forgot to set his alarm clocks and overslept or something."

Sam arrived
at Ed's house and
knocked on the little
wooden door.
There was no answer.

The rabbit knocked again.

Nothing.

He threw a few snowballs
at the bedroom window
and as there was still no
answer he opened
the door and
went into Ed's
kitchen.

The house
was very quiet, apart
from the steady ticking
of the kitchen clock.

Sam called Ed's name
and
went upstairs.

He opened
the bedroom
door
and went in.

There was Ed
smiling happily to himself,
fast asleep in bed, surrounded by soft
white pillows and his huge eiderdown.

Sam shook him gently
but Ed just snored
loudly and blew
out his
cheeks.

Sam poked Ed
and tickled
him

but
nothing
happened.

He shouted
close up to Ed's ear.
"Ed! Wake up,
it's morning
wake up!
Ed!"

Ed smiled happily on in oblivion.

Sam sighed, shrugged his shoulders

and went over to the
window.

Outside the sky was
a brilliant blue and
the white snow sparkled in the sun.
Sam felt disappointed. He knew that once
Ed had hibernated he could not be woken up.

All their hopes of
Ed winning the Free-Style
Ski Jump Championships
vanished. He turned from
the bright window to look
at Ed, rosy cheeked and
fast asleep, and smiled
sadly.

"He'll be so disappointed
when he wakes up in the
spring" Sam said aloud.

He vowed to make a
foolproof alarm system
for next year. The clocks, which Ed had
been too tired to set the night before,
ticked on quietly.

Sam walked over
the rush mats and out of the
bedroom door
shutting it gently behind him.

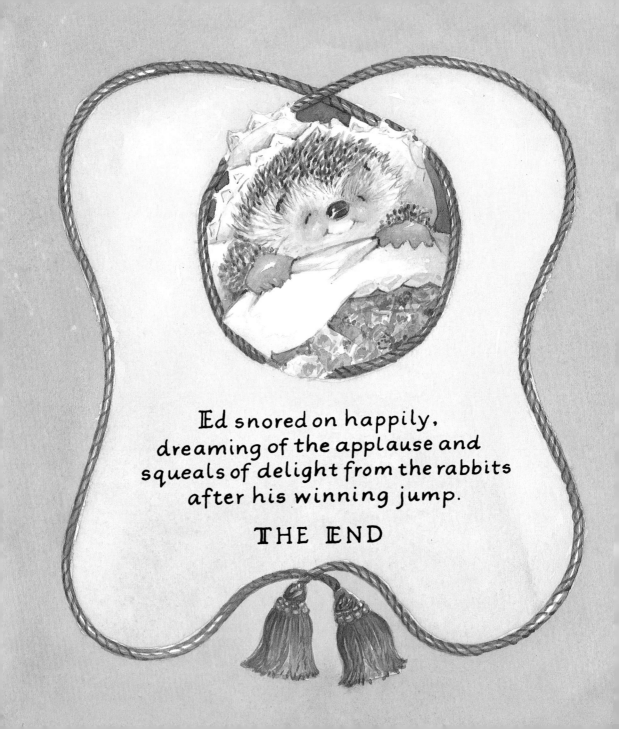

Ed snored on happily,
dreaming of the applause and
squeals of delight from the rabbits
after his winning jump.

THE END